Richard Scarry's
VROOMING, ZOOMING STORIES

A Random House PICTUREBACK® Book

RANDOM HOUSE 🏠 NEW YORK

Richard Scarry's A Day at the Airport © 2001 by Richard Scarry Corporation. *Richard Scarry's A Day at the Fire Station* © 2003 by Richard Scarry Corporation. *Richard Scarry's A Day at the Police Station* © 2004 by Richard Scarry Corporation. All rights reserved. Published in the United States by Random House Children's Books, a division of Penguin Random House LLC, New York, and in Canada by Penguin Random House Canada Limited, Toronto. The stories in this collection were originally published separately in the United States by Random House Children's Books, New York, in 2001, 2003, and 2004. Random House and the colophon are registered trademarks of Penguin Random House LLC.

Visit us on the Web!
randomhousekids.com
RichardScarryBooks.com

Educators and librarians, for a variety of teaching tools, visit us at RHTeachersLibrarians.com

Library of Congress Cataloging-in-Publication Data is available upon request.
ISBN 978-0-399-55592-3

Printed in the United States of America
10 9 8 7 6 5 4 3 2 1

Richard Scarry's
A DAY AT THE AIRPORT

Father Cat wants to take Huckle,
Sally, and Lowly out sailing this afternoon.
Plink! Plop! Plink!
Uh-oh, Father Cat, it's starting to rain.

He puts the
top up on the car.

"There's nothing to do but to go back home."

What a
disappointment.

Father Cat stops at Scotty's Filling Station for gasoline.
"Fill 'er up, please, Scotty!" Father Cat says.
Just then, Rudolf Von Flugel drives up in his airplane-car.
"Good afternoon, Father Cat!" says Rudolf. "Are you going sailing?"

"No, we're going home, Rudolf," Father Cat says sadly. "The children will have to play inside today."

"Hmm," says Rudolf. "Why don't they come with me? I'm going to the airport. There's lots to see there, even when it rains!"

"Wow! Can we, Dad?" Huckle asks.

Father Cat thinks it is a great idea. He helps place the children in Rudolf's airplane-car.

"Don't worry, Father Cat. I'll bring the children home dry as baked apple strudel!" says Rudolf.

And off they go! *Brruumm!*

radar

runway

pier

catering truck

control tower

catering kitchen

snowplow

airport bus

They arrive at the airport in no time.

wind sock

runway lights

hangar

a tractor towing a plane

restaurant

departure terminal

parking garage

ARRIVALS   DEPARTURES

arrivals

taxis

My, what a busy place it is!

check-in counters

TO PARIS ⬇

TO NEW YORK ⬇

TO VENICE ⬇

conveyor belt

scale

luggage cart

"Here we are!" Rudolf says, driving into the departure terminal.

CLOSED ✗

TO WORKVILLE ⬇

TO THE GATES ➡

Mind your head!!

luggage tag

DEPARTURES

	TIME	GATE
PARIS	3:30	2
WORK VILLE	4:00	1
VENICE	4:02	3
NEW YORK	5:15	1
LONDON	5:30	3
TOKYO	6:00	2

lots of luggage

porter

"These are the check-in counters. Passengers show their tickets here, and also have their baggage weighed and tagged with its destination," Rudolf explains. "Each passenger receives a boarding pass to enter the plane at the gate."

check-in hostess

ticket

boarding pass

"The airport terminal is like a small Busytown," says Rudolf. "There are shops that sell books, toys, and flowers. And there's a police station, a post office, and a first-aid center, too!"

"Is there a bathroom, Mr. Von Flugel?" Sally asks.

While they wait for Sally, Lowly asks if there is also a restaurant at the airport. "Travel always makes me thirsty!" he laughs.

As soon as Sally returns, Rudolf drives up the escalator to the restaurant.

restaurant

catering truck

boarding gate

WORKVILLE

passenger bus

kerosene fuel is pumped into tanks in the wings

baggage train

fire extinguisher

hose

cleaning truck

paper to recycle

bottles to recycle

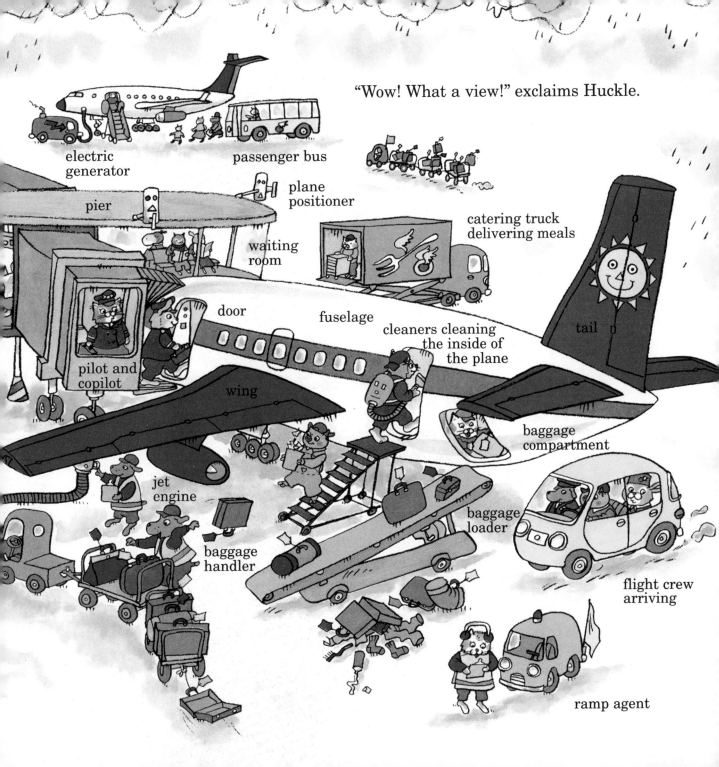

"Wow! What a view!" exclaims Huckle.

electric generator

passenger bus

pier

plane positioner

waiting room

catering truck delivering meals

door

fuselage

cleaners cleaning the inside of the plane

tail

pilot and copilot

wing

baggage compartment

jet engine

baggage loader

baggage handler

flight crew arriving

ramp agent

tractor

Rudolf drives over to the control tower.
Please take care driving up the stairs, Rudolf.

catering kitchen
preparing meals

searchlight

radio antenna

runway

binoculars

ground controller

a taxiing plane heading for the runway

control tower

follow-me car guiding landed airplanes

pilot studying the weather

FOLLOW ME

weatherman

in winter, snowplows clear the runways and taxiways

"From up here, each plane receives instructions by radio—where to park and when to take off and land," Rudolf explains. "At night and in fog, you can still see every plane on this radar screen."

DON'T STEP ON THE GRASS.

radar antenna

radar screen

"Busy Air Flight One, you're clear for takeoff," says the ground controller into the microphone.

The big plane races down the runway and soars into the sky. *Whooosh!*

Hey! No running on the runway!

wind sock showing the wind's direction

ground controller

"Mr. Von Flugel," says Sally, "you know so much. Can you tell me what that funny-looking thing over there is?"

Just a little to the right!

cargo plane

"Ach! I almost forgot!" cries Rudolf.
He drives across the runway, past a
cargo plane being loaded with freight
containers.

airplane hangars

luggage
trolleys

freight
containers

"These are the hangars,
Sally," says Rudolf. "Inside,
airplanes are parked and
repaired."

"Thank you, Mr. Von Flugel,"
Sally replies. "But what's *that*!?"
she asks, pointing.

"Ach! *This* is my Bratwurst Balloon!" Rudolf
says. "Quick! Hop in before you get wet!"

"Wow!"

"Look out, everyone!" calls the ground controller. "Here comes the Bratwurst Balloon!"

Soon they are high in the sky.

"Look! There's our house!" says Huckle.
"Mom! Dad! Look up!" he calls.

No, look *out,* Rudolf! Your Bratwurst Balloon is about to burst.

Bump! They all land safely on Huckle's front lawn.
"Well, Rudolf, that was a perfect landing," says Father Cat.
"Thank you, Mr. Von Flugel!" say Huckle, Sally, and Lowly.
"This has been the best afternoon ever!"

Richard Scarry's
A DAY AT THE FIRE STATION

"Wonderful!" replies
Chief Smokey.

Drippy and Sticky, the housepainters,
pull up in front of the Busytown fire station.
"We're here to paint the firehouse!"
says Drippy.

"But please don't park your paint truck in front of the firehouse doors," Smokey says. "We firefighters have to be able to drive out at ANY time."

After parking their paint truck
out of the way, Drippy and Sticky
enter the fire station.

"Wow! What a nifty place!" says Drippy.

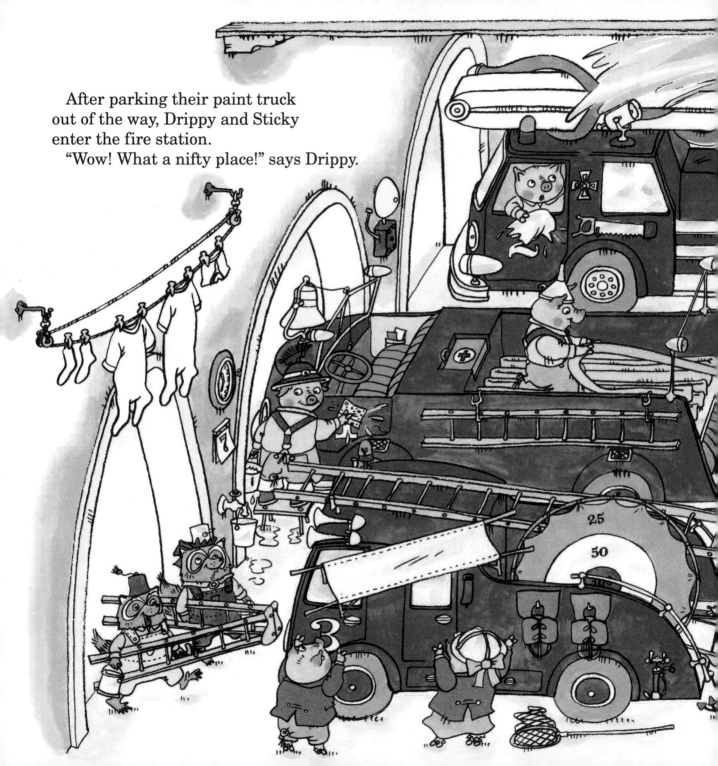

The firefighters are busy cleaning their fire engines.
"We firefighters like to keep our engines nice and clean,
so please be careful not to get any paint on them,"
says Smokey.

"Aye-aye, sir!" replies Sticky.

Drippy covers a fire engine with a big cloth so that it won't get dripped on. Sticky opens the cans of paint.

Drippy begins to paint the firehouse ceiling pink. Sticky starts to paint the firehouse poles in candy stripes.

Oops! Drippy's cloth seems to have slipped off the fire engine.

"My red fire engine!" shouts Smokey. "It's pink!"

"Don't worry," says Drippy. "We'll have your fire engine cleaned up in no time."

But instead of rubbing off, the wet paint smears in long streaks. What a mess!

RRRINNG! RRRINNG! sounds a loud bell. It's the fire station alarm!

The firefighters sleeping in the dormitory upstairs leap from their beds and slide down the poles to the engines below.

"Oh, no!" shout Drippy and Sticky.
"Oh, no!" shout the firefighters,
covered in candy-stripe paint.

But stained uniforms or no, the brave firefighters jump into their boots, grab their coats and helmets, and charge out of the fire station aboard their red—and pink— fire engines. WWWRRRR! CLANG! CLANG!

"Well," says Drippy, "now that the firefighters are gone, perhaps we can get our painting done."

The firefighters have been called out to a traffic accident. Cecelia's cement mixer bumped into Horace's honey truck and knocked over Farmer Hal's haywagon. What a gooey mess!

Thank goodness for the firefighters! They will have everything cleaned up in no time.

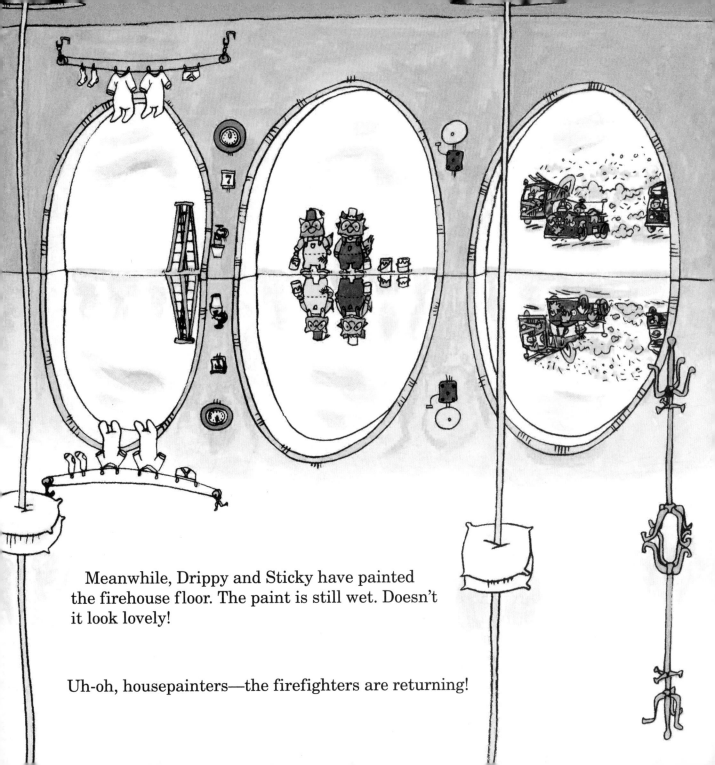

Meanwhile, Drippy and Sticky have painted the firehouse floor. The paint is still wet. Doesn't it look lovely!

Uh-oh, housepainters—the firefighters are returning!

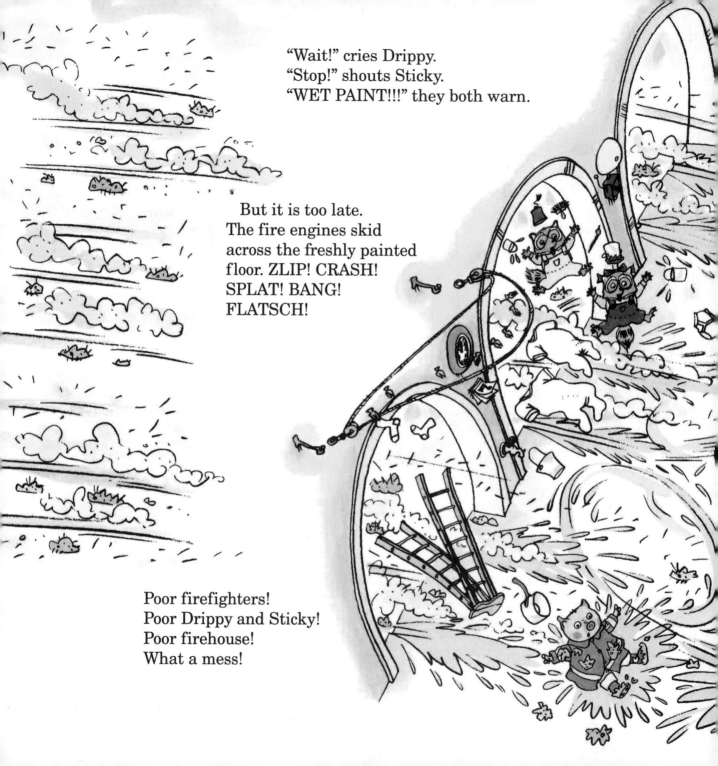

"Wait!" cries Drippy.
"Stop!" shouts Sticky.
"WET PAINT!!!" they both warn.

But it is too late.
The fire engines skid
across the freshly painted
floor. ZLIP! CRASH!
SPLAT! BANG!
FLATSCH!

Poor firefighters!
Poor Drippy and Sticky!
Poor firehouse!
What a mess!

Straw and cement and honey are EVERYWHERE.

Smokey picks up a hose and sprays out the fire station. SWWIIIIIIIIISH! SWWOOOOOSH!

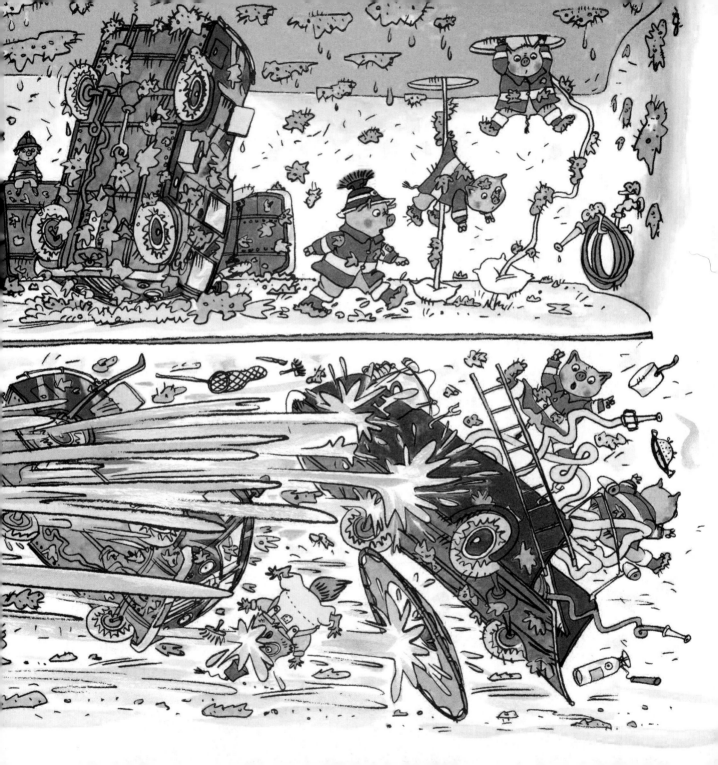

Suddenly, there is another alarm.
This time, it's a fire!

The firefighters throw all their equipment
into the fire engines and are off to the rescue.

Look! It's a fire at Vesuvio's Peppery Pizza Parlor!
The firefighters quickly hook up the pumper engine
to the fire hydrant and bravely rush inside.

The fire is in the oven! (It's a burnt pizza.)
Hurry, firefighters!
With a spray of water from the hose, the fire is put out.

To thank the firefighters, Vesuvio invites
them all to a big pizza lunch. Isn't he nice?

Meanwhile, Drippy and Sticky have finished repainting the firehouse.

The firefighters bring Drippy and Sticky a take-away pizza, and wash their fire engines OUTSIDE the fire station while the fresh paint dries. Aren't they thoughtful?

Just then, Tammy Tapir drives up in her strawberry jam truck.

"Can anyone please tell me how to get to the thruway from here?" Tammy asks the firefighters.

Uh-oh. Isn't that Roger Rhino's wrecking crane coming?

Hey, slow down there, Roger!

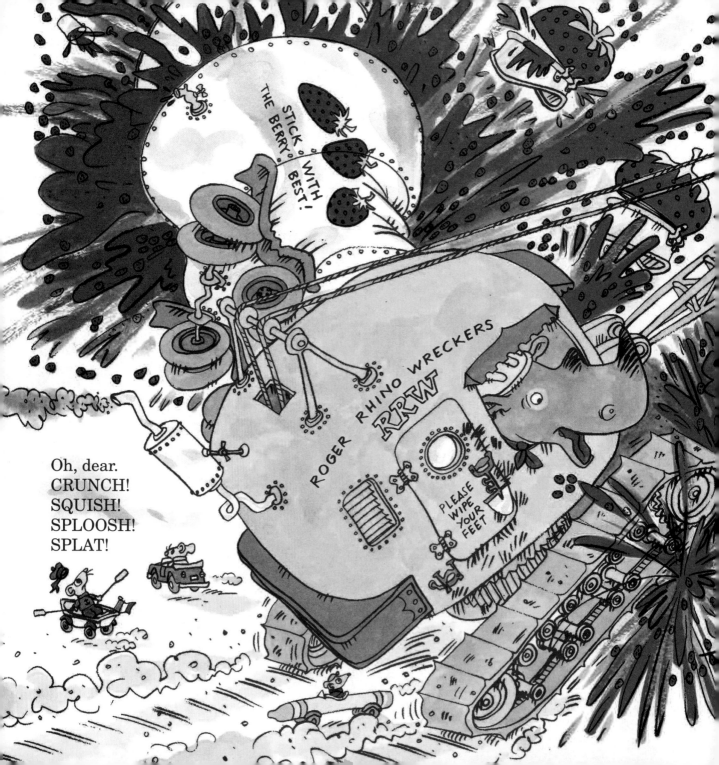

Nice work, Roger!

"Gee, I'm awfully sorry about this," says Roger, apologizing. "Oh, don't worry," says Smokey with a sigh. "We'll have this cleaned up in no time. It's all in a firefighter's day at the fire station."

Richard Scarry's
A DAY AT THE
POLICE STATION

It is Friday evening.
The Murphy family has finished
dinner. Mrs. Murphy clears the table
while Sergeant Murphy washes
the dishes.

"It's time to get into your
pajamas and go off to bed,"
Mrs. Murphy tells Bridget.

"Run along up to your room and I'll read
you a story!" calls Sergeant Murphy.

While Bridget climbs the stairs, she can hear her parents talking in the kitchen.

"I have to go to Workville tomorrow, Sarge," says Mrs. Murphy. "Could you please look after Bridget?"

"Hmmm," replies Sergeant Murphy. "Officer Flo is sick. I have to be on duty for her tomorrow—but I'll just take Bridget to the police station with me. She won't mind, I think."

But when Sergeant Murphy goes up to Bridget's room, he finds her crying.

"What's the matter, Bridget?" Sergeant Murphy asks.

"I wanted to go to the amusement park tomorrow," Bridget cries. "And now you have to work! I don't like that you're a police officer. You're ALWAYS on duty!"

"But being a police officer is very important," says Sergeant Murphy, hugging Bridget. "I'm sorry we can't go to the amusement park, but we'll have a good time at the police station. THAT I can promise!"

The next morning,
Sergeant Murphy and Bridget
drive off to the police station.
"Goodbye, Bridget!" calls
Mrs. Murphy. "Goodbye, Sarge!"

On the way, they
come to an intersection.
There is a huge traffic jam!
The traffic light
is broken.

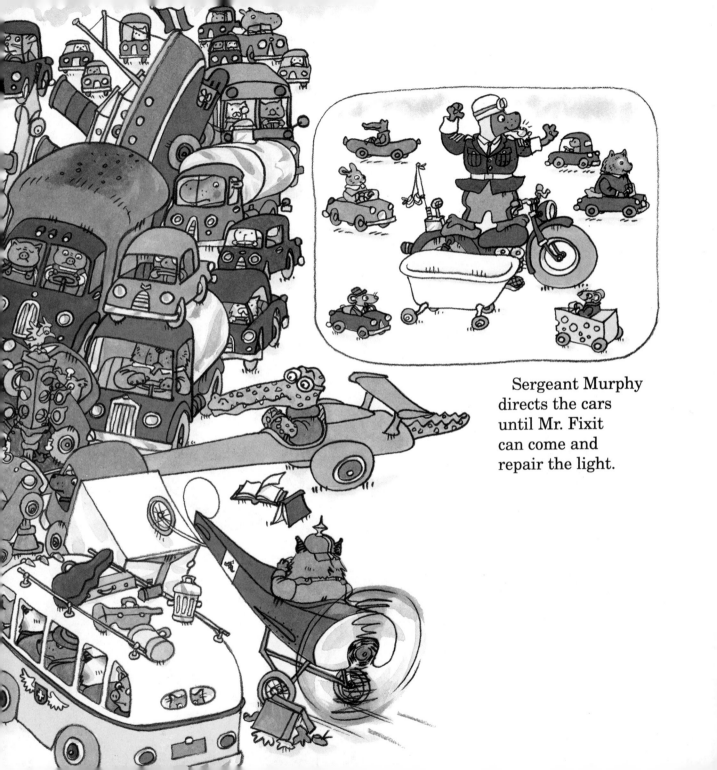

Sergeant Murphy
directs the cars
until Mr. Fixit
can come and
repair the light.

"This is what Daddy calls
a good time?" Bridget says, pouting.
"Watching traffic?"

Just then, Mr. Raccoon
comes out of his coffee shop,
bringing Bridget a glass
of milk and a donut.

"Your father sure does a great job, Bridget!" he says.
"I don't know what Busytown would do without him."

Soon Sergeant Murphy and Bridget are on their way again. When they arrive at the police station, the telephone is ringing.

Sergeant Murphy answers it. "Busytown police station. Sergeant Murphy here."

It's Hilda Hippo on the line.

"Oh, Sergeant Murphy, I'm so frightened!
There's a ghost in my bathroom!"
"A GHOST?" Sergeant Murphy replies.
"Just stay calm, Hilda. I'll be right over!"

Sergeant Murphy
and Bridget race over to Hilda's.

When they arrive, Hilda looks
as pale as a ghost herself.

"Sergeant Murphy, I haven't
slept a wink!" Hilda says
nervously. "The ghost has been
flushing the toilet all night!"

Suddenly, from
upstairs comes:
FLUSH!

"Hmmm," says Sergeant Murphy.
"You two wait here while I
see about this—er—ghost."

He peeks inside,
but the bathroom
is empty.

FLUSH!
goes the toilet again.
Sergeant Murphy
climbs onto the toilet
seat and checks inside
the tank.

"There!" he says.

"The toilet just needed some
adjusting. You shouldn't let your
imagination run away with you
like that, Hilda!"

On the way back to the police station, they
see a toddler crying in the street.

Sergeant Murphy takes her to the police station.

The phone is ringing when they
arrive. It's the child's mother!
Thank goodness her darling is safe
with Sergeant Murphy. Bridget
plays with the toddler until
her mother comes to fetch her.

Just then, Mr. Frumble arrives at the door. "Excuse me, but has anyone seen my hat?" he asks. "It's the third one I've lost in three days!"

Sergeant Murphy makes a note of the lost hat and promises to call Mr. Frumble if it's found.

Minutes after Mr. Frumble leaves, Mr. Gronkle storms in.

"I'm here to report a robbery!" he shouts.

"Wow! A real robbery!" thinks Bridget.

"My car keys have been stolen," says Mr. Gronkle, "and I know who took them: Wolfgang Wolf, Harry Hyena, and Benny Baboon!"

Through the door come Wolfgang, Harry, and Benny—each wearing a green hat.

"Did somebody call us?" asks Wolfgang.

"We found these hats," says Harry.

"And we're bringing them here to be returned to their rightful owner!" adds Benny.

"I saw you thieves walking around my car," shouts Mr. Gronkle. "You must have stolen my keys! I can't find them anywhere!"

"Now, just a moment, Mr. Gronkle!" Sergeant Murphy says. "You have to have some proof before you can accuse someone of stealing."

"We didn't take your keys!" says Wolfgang.

"We'd never steal anything!" says Harry.

"Honest!" adds Benny.

Sergeant Murphy decides they should all go together to the scene of the crime.

"Are THESE your stolen keys?" Bridget asks Mr. Gronkle, holding up a ring of keys.

"Why, yes!" replies Mr. Gronkle, surprised. "Wherever did you find them?"

"Under your car, by the door," says Bridget.

"I guess your 'thief' must have accidentally dropped them," Sergeant Murphy tells Mr. Gronkle.

"I owe you an apology," Mr. Gronkle says to Wolfgang, Harry, and Benny. "To make up for my mistake, I want to take you out for sundaes."

As they walk back to the police station, Sergeant Murphy and Bridget see two boys fighting.

Sergeant Murphy runs up and pulls them apart. "Stop that!" he says. "What's this all about?"

"Jimmy won't let me ride his bike!" says Johnny.
"It's MY bike!" shouts Jimmy.

"You need to settle your problems peacefully," Sergeant Murphy tells the boys.

Just then, Bridget hears someone crying, "HELP!"

Sergeant Murphy races
to the edge of the pier.
He bravely dives into
the river!

Sergeant Murphy carries
Bananas Gorilla safely out of
the river.
My, isn't he strong!

Then he dives back into the river!
Does he want to go for a swim?

No! He wants to get
Bananas's Bananamobile!
"Please do be careful
when driving near the water,"
Sergeant Murphy tells
Bananas.

Back at the police
station, Sergeant Murphy
puts on a dry uniform.
"We have to hurry, or we'll
be late for school!" he says.

Bridget is confused.
"School? On Saturday?" she wonders.

Sergeant Murphy and Bridget arrive at the school playground. Some children have come with their bikes for a traffic safety class.

Here are some of the things Sergeant Murphy teaches them:

Ride single file.

Always obey traffic lights and signals.

Give hand signals when turning.

Cross the street at the crosswalk.

Wear a helmet!

Make sure your brakes, lights, and bell work properly.

And please don't leave your bike lying around.

Park it properly. Thank you!

"We missed you at the amusement park today, Bridget," Huckle says.
"I was on duty with Daddy all day!" Bridget replies. "We got rid of a ghost and helped a little girl find her mommy. Then we solved a robbery, and Daddy stopped two boys who were fighting. Then he bravely saved Bananas Gorilla from drowning!"

"Wow!" says Huckle. "Having a dad who's a police officer must be pretty neat!"

"You bet it is!" replies Bridget. "I think my daddy has the very best job EVER!"

"Um—excuse me, Sergeant Murphy, but has anyone seen my hat yet?"